Allan Patrick Judd

Adventures of Buddy The Blimp

FIRST FLIGHT

First published by AuthorHouse 11/03/05

ISBN: 1-4208-5937-4 (sc)

Printed in the United States of America
Bloomington, Indiana

This book is printed on acid-free paper.

authorHOUSE

1663 LIBERTY DRIVE
BLOOMINGTON, INDIANA 47403
(800) 839-8640
www.authorhouse.com

Buddy's story is dedicated to the children of the world
and the child in all of us.

THIS BOOK IS GIVEN TO: *Angelo*

BY: *Scott & Kathy*

OCCASION: *Merry Christmas*

SENTIMENT: *2018*

Special thanks to my mother who, when I was a little guy, taught me to believe in myself and pursue my dreams.

CHAPTER ONE

MY FIRST FRIEND

It is early in the morning, a time when all the birds are still asleep.
A mist hugs the ground as if to say, "I am your blanket."
Above, the stars are twinkling. Down low in the eastern sky, a thin blue line
is beginning to appear.

Inside my home, in the quiet of dawn, a low rumble suddenly turns into a roar as a huge vertical split appears in the wall in front of me. Frightened by the noise and amazed at the unfolding view beyond the hangar doors, I look for my ground crew. They have been with me since my first memories and do not seem scared at all. Rather, a sense of excitement fills the air as I float gently above the floor. Some of them are holding my whiskers and others move around the hangar beneath me.

Here comes a fellow wearing a white shirt with small black and silver lines on his shoulders. He stops to speak with a crewman standing under my nose, then approaches and disappears under my belly. Where did he go I wonder? After a moment, I feel myself settle to the hangar floor. The crewman in front of me signals the others and I move slowly towards the large opening.

Slipping through the doors into my new life I come to a stop, well clear of
the hangar. The air feels cooler. It is not as cozy as it was inside.
Suddenly I hear my crew cheer,
"Hip-hip hooray, BUDDY the BLIMP has come out to play."

As night becomes day, the stars begin to fade and the colors of the sky near the horizon become red, orange and pink.

An early morning bird, Lovey the Dove notices all the activity outside the hangar and decides to investigate.

As she streaks towards me out of the morning light, I find my voice, "Hey, what are you and how do you move around like that?"

"I am a bird and I learned to fly when I was very young. My name is Lovey Dovey but my friends just call me Dove. You must be BUDDY."

"How did you know my name?" I ask.

"Well, you can't miss it. It's written on your sides."

The ground crew let go of my whiskers as I lift from the ground. "I am unsure of myself floating out here. Will you stay and keep me company Dove?"

"Sure Buddy, it would be fun. You really are BIG, yet you seem as light as one of my feathers."

An orange-yellow sun is rising and starts to warm my skin. I sense a force building inside as I begin some serious humming. "This is very strange." My ground crew waves me off as I slowly move towards the field.

"Wow, I'm up in the air! I feel a bit dizzy. Am I supposed to be doing this?"
Dove thinks he may be in trouble. He's heading straight for a tree. "Buddy,
LOOK OUT! Come up here into the open sky."

"I was so caught up in floating along I wasn't watching where I was going."

"Buddy, these trees reach for the sky and they hold onto the ground really tight with their roots. If you crash into one, both you and the tree will get hurt. So when you are near the earth, be sure to look out for obstacles and point yourself so you won't hit anything."

"That sounds like a good idea. I'll remember that Dove." As I climb away, everything begins to look smaller. "What a ride!" Towards the sunrise, the colors are very different and silvery. Higher than the hangar, the air seems much warmer. Being up here will take some getting used to. I am all at once, so nervous and excited. At least my new friend is here with me.

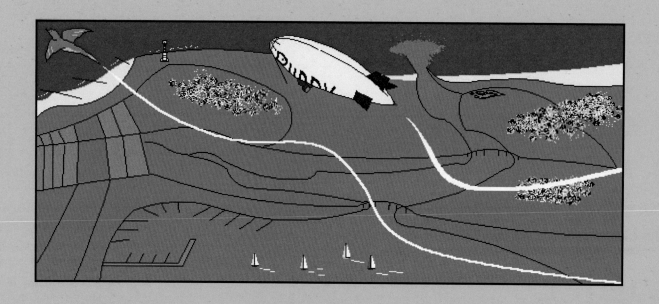

As I follow Dove way into the sky, it seems I can point my nose up and down, left and right, whenever I feel like it. Now that I gain confidence in my ability to steer, I become more comfortable with the height. The mist covering the fields below is dissipating but still clings to little pockets of trees.

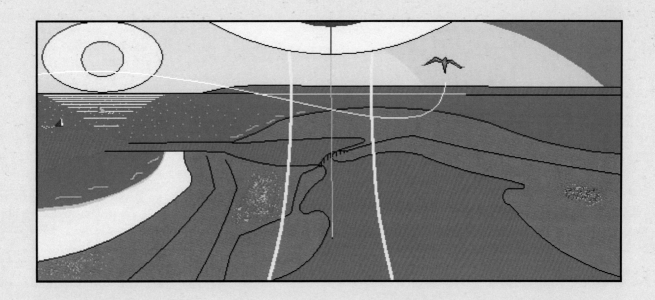

In the distance, I can see the shoreline and the bright yellow sun shimmering on the waves. As we climb further into the sky, my skin tightens. "I don't feel so good!!"

Perhaps Buddy is a little frightened way up here for the first time, Dove thinks to herself. "Let's go back down and look for my friend Sam the seagull. He is a smart old seabird who loves to tell stories about the ocean."

"Ok, let's go."

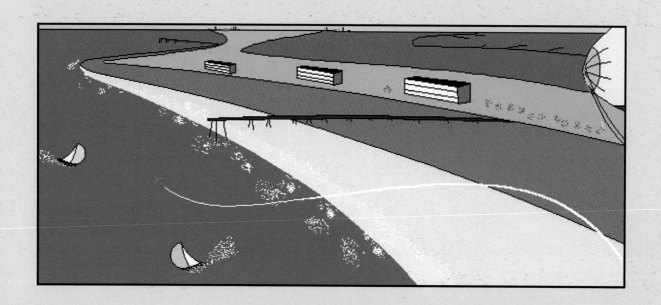

To descend, I point my nose down but it doesn't stay there. It seems to want to level off. Maybe I should try harder. At least my skin isn't as tight anymore. Here we go...... Now I feel better. I am pointing right at the beach but somehow not speeding up like Dove. I can't keep up with her. I wonder why?

She is already way down there. What an awesome view! "What is this beneath us? It all seems to be moving in one direction."

"What you see is water and waves of energy passing by. See where it loses its clarity and becomes a vivid mix of colors?"

"Yes I do!"

"That's the shore break."

Still descending, things start to look bigger again. As I level off, I hear something coming from below. "Dove, what am I hearing and what is all this white stuff?"

"Well, the swooshing is made by the waves running aground, breaking and rolling until their energy is shared with the land. The white trails are a combination of seaspray, bubbles and foam. Air flowing over water disturbs the surface and creates waves that can travel far until finally, they come ashore in the most rhythmic sound."

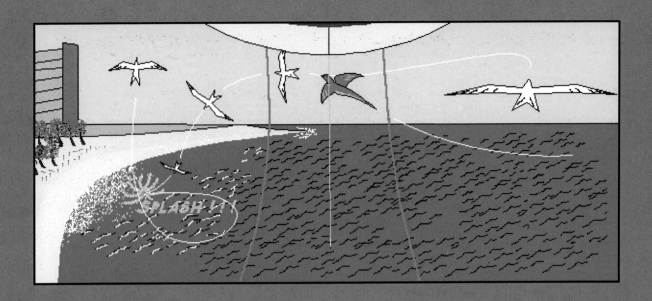

I am cruising so low my whiskers are almost touching the waves. White birds with black wingtips fly gracefully by. Occasionally, they turn quickly and dive into the water, then pop back up with something silvery wiggling in their mouths. With a little shake of their wings, they take off again. "Why are those birds doing that?"

"They're feeding on tiny fish to maintain flying strength for the day."

Oh, I have so much to learn.

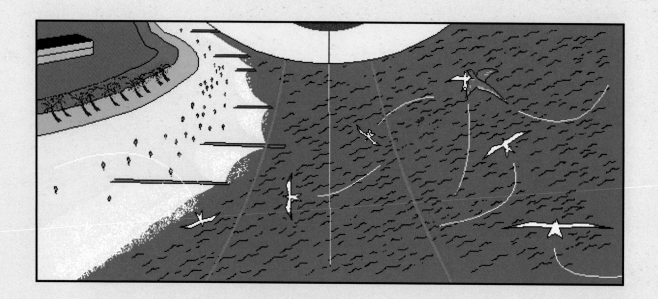

Up the beach, I notice little people who wave and run all over the place.
Others are just standing there.

    "Buddy, let's go see if we can find that old seagull."

    "Does he look like these birds?"

    "Yes he does and we should find him beyond the pier near the inlet where
he dives for fish."

    "Great!"

"And what are all these tall and skinny looking trees with large leaves and round things hanging underneath? What are they Dove?"

She laughs at my ignorance. "Coconut Palms of course!"

I like this place. The air, the ocean and the land all come together in such a beautiful way.

CHAPTER TWO

MY FLOATING OCEAN FRIENDS

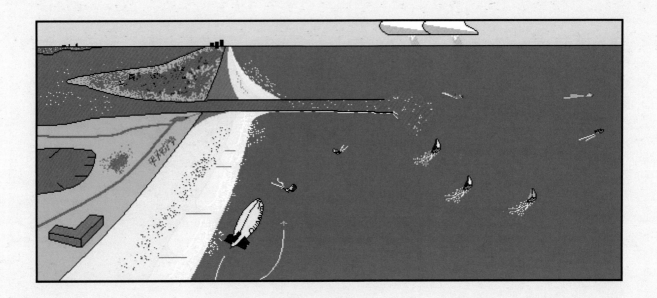

Cruising along the beach close to the waves, we approach the jetty. "There's so much to see here Dove!"

"Yes Buddy, the shoreline is one of my favorite places."

"What are all those things moving around on the water?"
"They are some of our floating friends. The quiet ones catch the wind with their sails and are called sailboats. The noisy ones hum along like you. They are powerboats."

"A warm sunny day brings them out to play on the ocean, as we do in the air. Oh here's Sam at the end of the jetty, on the channel marker!"

I can see him proudly surveying his territory.

"Good morning Dove," squawks the old seagull, "I've been watching you come up the beach. Who is this new buddy following you? He reminds me of someone I know but I can't quite put my wingtip on it."

"Funny you'd say that Sam. His name is Buddy. I found him floating by
the old hangar. He looks like our friend Echo Dolphin, but so much bigger."
"Hello there Buddy!   I've never seen anything quite like you before.
What are you?"

"Let me think. You are Big! You appear to be Light in the air. The way you move is Impressive. You seem Majestic and must be Pleasant or Dove wouldn't be with you. Could you be a BLIMP? That's it! You ARE a BLIMP! 'BUDDY THE BLIMP'."

"Gee! I remember the crew calling me this earlier. So I am a BLIMP!
It's great to meet you Sam. Dove told me you know a lot about the ocean.
You must love this place. It takes my breath away!"
                              "And so do YOU!"

I feel warm all over. Could it be the sunshine? No, it's something different. Is this what it feels like to be accepted simply for who you are?

"You make me feel so welcome. Is this how friends feel about each other?"

"Yes Buddy, it is one of the nicest feelings I know," says the old seagull, pausing to reflect...... "Do you want to meet Wind Gust the sailboat? You'll like the way he moves."

"Ok, let's go find him."

Jumping off the channel marker, Sam and Dove head towards the beach. Picking up speed, I follow them over the waves.

For the first time, I notice my shadow. It is large. Some of the water is really clear with such lovely colors and patterns in it. "This is pure magic."

Gliding past the boats, Sam catches sight of Wind Gust below.

"Hi Windy! Nice day for sailing, what?"

"It is! There's a pleasant breeze down here. Who's your big friend?"

"He's 'Buddy the Blimp.' He loves to move low and slow."

"I see that!"

"Buddy, meet Wind Gust. He's number 2, the one with the yellow sail."

I call down to greet him. "Hi, what are you doing?"

"I'm racing, catching the wind. I say old chap, how do you stay up in the air like that?"

"I don't know, but it does feel nice. Sam, do you know?"

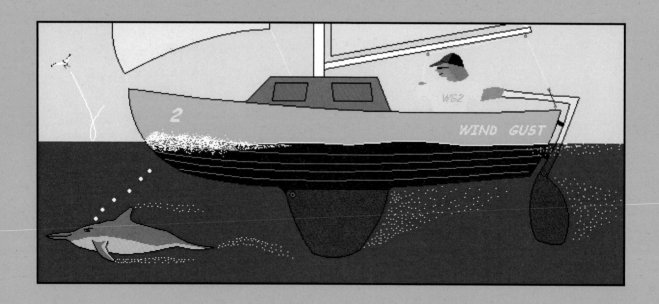

In order to explain, the old seagull asks Windy, "How do you feel when you are on the beach and the breeze fills your sails?"

"Well, I want to move but the solid ground won't give way. I feel stuck, like the sand is holding me back. But now that I am in the water, I slip through it with ease because I am floating."

"That's right Windy. Just like me when I dive for fish. I am so light the water lifts me up. BLIMP is buoyant just like you and I."

"Oh. Now I get it."

Sam continues, "The air around Buddy is doing the same thing."

"So, he's floating in it like the submarines in the ocean right?"

"Yep, that's it Windy."

As I listen to them speak, my first day starts to make sense.

Now I wonder how Dove and the old seabird stay up in the air. "How do you keep from falling out of the sky? How do you fly Sam?"

"The idea is to have enough air moving past my wings to get lift. I can either glide with them stretched out at an angle or flap to move air back and down with each stroke."

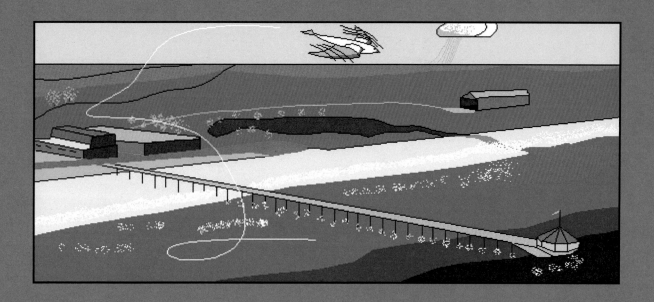

"To climb against gravity I must work very hard, but descending is easy and fun! Then I don't have to flap my wings and the steeper I glide the faster I go. The fastest is straight down. I use that one for catching fish." Satisfied with his explanation, he swoops around.

Now I begin to understand what makes him fly.

Wind Gust is falling behind in the race. "By golly," he hollers, "I must catch more wind to keep up. Here I go! Hey, watch me Buddy, I'm really moving now!"

"Wow, look at you lean!"

The breeze is really pushing his sails but what is pushing me through the air I wonder? "Why do I gain speed when I hum more?"

"Buddy, you're always thinking," Sam remarks. "You will go a long way with questions like that. Have you noticed that the powerboats hum like you do?"

"Yes I have and this one below is loud."

After a deep breath, the old seagull starts to describe what he observed when he too was very young and curious."

"Once when I was diving for fish behind a boat, I saw two strange looking things. One of them was spinning, moving water towards me. The other was stopped and looked like it had wings. I realized that if they both hummed a lot, they could really push that powerboat forward. As I popped out of the water and climbed back into the air, I asked him what his name was. 'Props' he said. And what those spinning wings underneath were? With a grin, he answered that since they propel him, of course they must be called 'propellers'."

"Buddy, yours look like the one on my friend Thrusty the Airplane. Since he can't flap his wings, he has to spin his propeller to accelerate until he moves fast enough for his wings to lift him off the ground. To maintain flying speed he must keep on humming unless he wants to descend with gravity in a quiet glide."

"Right now, your propellers are spinning slowly but you should still be able to feel the air flowing under your belly and tickling your lower tail fin."

"Yes I do now that you mention it."

    "Great. The way you are floating reminds me of a birthday balloon I once saw drifting up into the sky. I remember the father explaining to his daughter upset about losing her balloon that it went up because the air around it was heavier than the helium inside. Now I realize that you too must be filled with it."

    "Oh, what a gas!"

"Hey, since I'm just hanging around, how about a ride?"
  "What a great idea!! Let's go."
  Sam and Dove land on my tail, stretch their wings, then tuck them away.
  "Hey Blimp, this slow cruise sure beats flapping all day!"

As we drift along, the warm wind occasionally ruffles one of their feathers. Dove preens herself gently in the light breeze and the old seagull settles into a comfortable nap in the glowing sunshine, feeling completely at ease with my steadiness. It is nice to be with such trusting friends.

CHAPTER THREE

THE CLEAR BLUE SEA

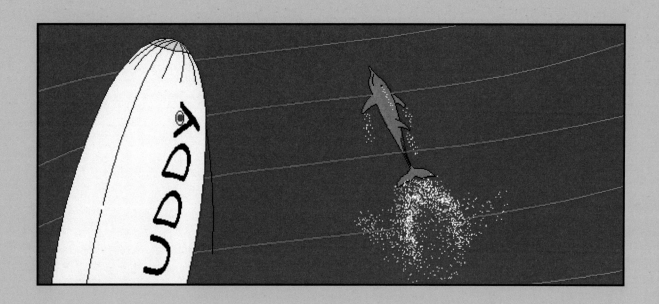

The waves rise over the sandbar into shallow water where they trip gracefully forward, leaving a light salt mist in the air. Under me, a streamlined shape is moving effortlessly in the clear blue sea. What could it be I wonder?

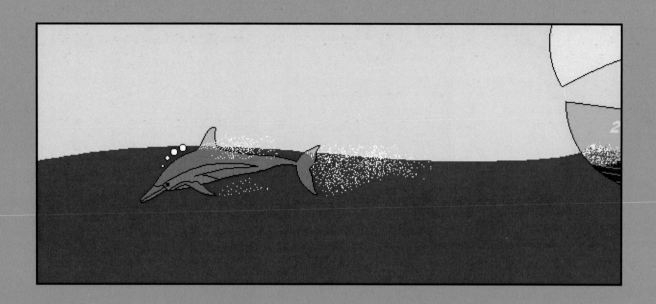

Every time it breaks the surface and bubbles escape from its blowhole, white foam is left behind. I must find out!

The old seagull is fast asleep on my tail next to Dove. "Hey Sam, wake up! I have another question for you. Who's that in the water?"

"Huh. Oh. Hang on Buddy. Give me a second to clear my head."

His feathers ruffle in the passing breeze as he opens his wings. Setting their angle to catch the wind, he lifts off, then glides by my side and looks around.

"Oh, that's Echo the Dolphin. She is one of the smartest creatures in the ocean."

Dove and Sam dive low over the waves. Noticing them above, Echo turns sharply and joyfully jumps into the air.

"Wow, nice move Echo!" shouts Buddy.

Echo splashes back into the water, spins around and looks up at us. "Dove, look at the whale floating in the sky!"

"That's our friend Buddy the Blimp," she laughs.

"Eeee," she squeaks, "He also looks like the submarines I sometimes play with, except upside down. Buddy, can you stop like they do and hover?"

"Hover? I'm not sure. Maybe I can if I slow my hum and lean back a bit." I feel that light tickle of air moving forward under my belly. As I slow down my whiskers start to hang straight down. "Look! I'm completely stopped and not sinking or rising. I've done it! This is great! Now I remember doing this hovering thing when I first lifted off."

"Echo, I saw you turning left and right down there. What were you doing?"

"I was searching for fish while my family played by the sandbar."

"You were releasing air a minute ago, in a big circle."

"Yes, I blow a curtain of bubbles to trap the fish inside and then I catch them in my mouth."

"How clever!"

Smiling, she says, "I would love to spend more time with you Buddy, but for now, I must keep on fishing. Enjoy your hovering." She turns her head and swims off into the waves.

"Sam, she looks so strong and yet so gentle."
"She is the ocean's health guardian and her ability to think is incredible. Some members of her family spend time teaching people to speak 'Dolphin'. One day, they will."

Listening to the old seagull talk about Echo's family, I get a strange sensation inside. What could it be? All of a sudden I feel like heading back to my hangar. "I want to go home."

"Maybe that's a good idea," Dove says. "By now, you must be getting low on energy and a bit hungry Buddy. When you get back, you'll be glad to be with your ground crew."

"It has been fun playing with you and meeting your friends. I can't wait to see you again. So long for now."

"So long."

As I turn and head towards shore, I seem to be going a lot faster than before. I must be cruising along with the wind. This is neat!

"There he goes," says Dove. "Sam, do you think I should fly along with him to make sure he doesn't lose his way?"

"Nope! He needs to follow his bearings so he can learn to trust himself. This, he must do on his own! It will be great experience for him."

    As I cross the shore, suddenly I realize that I am alone and a little frightened, yet I feel strangely calm, like something inside is guiding me. I begin to recognize some of the things I saw in the early morning light on my way to the beach with Dove.

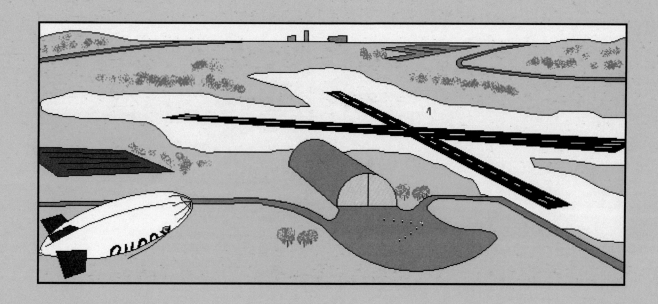

Hey, there's my home! It's huge compared to everything else in the distance. It truly stands out! The air is much warmer here than it was over the ocean. Rising bubbles swirl around, pushing me up, down, left and sideways. I must concentrate on moving my tail fins in order to keep myself going straight.

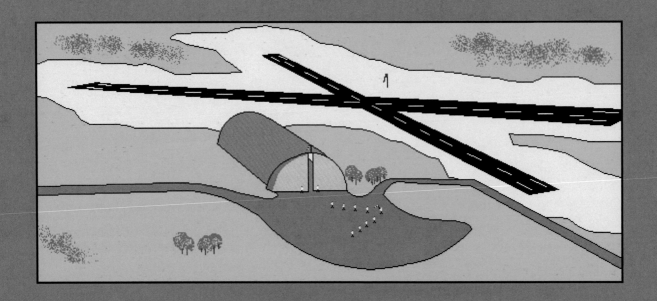

The hangar doors begin to open slowly. My ground crew is now clearly visible below, forming two straight lines like open arms waiting for me to enter. Ok, how do I get down there while missing those trees and stopping right where the crew is? I have an idea.

In my mind, I imagine a line starting below, curving to avoid the obstacles and coming up to me. Now that I see it, I begin my descent. But because of the swirling air, I must keep humming until final approach. When I don't need to anymore, then I can hover into the arms of my crew. That's a plan! But what if my whiskers miss them? I guess I could go around and try again. I sure hope this works out. As I finish the turn, whoa, air currents push me sideways towards the trees! Oh Ooh! That's what Dove warned me about. Quick, I need more humming! PHEW! That was close!

Time to stop and hover! I think I've got it! As I slow down, my ground crew grab my whiskers, separating them to each side of my nose. The last two fellows walk under my belly.

"Welcome back home Buddy," yells JB.

Wow, no crewman has ever spoken to me before! "Oh yes, it is so nice to be back! I am glad I made it!"

"For a first, that was a nice approach. We will now tug you over to the mooring mast and attach your nose to it. While we do, keep it directly over my head and watch for any changes in wind direction. Once you are securely attached we can relax, but jump back into the sky if we lose control of you."

"Ok, but I sure hope you don't!"

I can see another crewman on top of the mooring mast. As I get closer, he vanishes from sight. After some tugging, pushing and pulling, my nose bumps gently and clicks into place. I could not have done this alone. In a gesture of friendship, the mast-headsman greets me with a tap, "At-a-boy!"

My ground crew and the mast truck immediately maneuver me tail first into the hangar. This appears a bit tricky, but what a beautiful thing to watch. It feels very cozy being inside my home again.

JB says, "There is someone you need to meet Buddy. He is very much a part of you."

Who is he I wonder?

Now I see him! It's the fellow with stripes on his shoulders. He looks up and shouts, "Hey Now! I am your Captain and you are a mighty Airship."

I was astonished by the zeal of this individual. "My Captain? I have a Captain? What's your name?"

"My name is Mr. Breeze. Did you enjoy your first flight with me?"

"It was incredible and I made lots of friends, but I wasn't sure about anything I was doing at first."

"Buddy, you took to the air like dolphins take to the ocean."

"Now I know it was you helping me out Captain Breeze. I felt more at ease as the day progressed. Something inside was guiding me it seemed."

"Buddy, that's what having faith and believing in yourself is all about."

I really like this fellow.

"As a little boy, I dreamed of floating low and slow above the treetops," explains the captain. "Now I can. With YOU! Otherwise it would be an impossible feat to achieve by myself. I'm too heavy to float in the air on my own and you are too young to go out by yourself without possibly getting lost and hurt. But together as buddies, we can go above the earth and share new horizons."

"Now rest your props and get some sleep. Your pressure watchman will keep you safe until morning. When you wake up, we will see how much farther we can safely go. Thanks for the ride Buddy and good night."

   His words and manner of command leave me speechless and deep in reflective thought about the events of the day. As I float gently, the cooling air reminds me of early this morning when I went out to play. The sky is fast changing colors with various streaks and shades as the effortless spin of the earth turns us deeper into the night, bringing out the twinkling stars. Safe again with my family, I drift off to sleep.

THE END

BOOK ONE

GLOSSARY

The <u>Captain</u> pilots the Airship (Blimp). He is also the person responsible for managing the entire support team of people and for managing the flight operations of the Blimp.

The <u>Ground Crew Chief</u> is the person responsible for organizing all the ground activities associated with the Blimp. He also gives hand signals to his crewmembers in order to move it around on the ground, during the launching, landing and docking maneuvers.

The <u>Mast-headsman</u> is the person responsible for receiving the nose of the Blimp and connecting it securely to the top of the mast called the "mast head". Without him and his fellow ground crew members, a Blimp cannot be anchored and therefore must continue flying. They are essential to the operation of any Airship.

A <u>Hangar</u> is a big building where Blimps, Planes and Helicopters can go inside and sleep.

The <u>Mooring</u> is like an anchor for a Boat. It is designed to keep the nose of the Blimp in one place so the tail weather vanes freely with any wind changes just as a Boat does when the tide changes. The <u>mooring</u> can be a pole, mast or a truck with a telescopic mast, but in either case, once positioned, they are held firmly in place by cables attached to long pegs called 'stakes' driven or screwed into the ground.

<u>Floating</u> occurs when an object doesn't sink or rise when immersed in a fluid. That condition is known as 'Equilibrium'. Buddy weighs 10,000 pounds. That's five tons! He floats at equilibrium in the air because his 'lighter-than-air helium" filled balloon is holding aside 10,000 pounds of air. He wants you to try something! The next time you have a birthday balloon handy, hold it down, cut the ribbon and let the plastic weight fall to the floor. Then, tie a bow in the ribbon and begin adding paperclips to it. At first, it will still rise because the helium filled balloon is holding aside air that weighs more than the combined weight of the balloon, ribbon and paperclips. Keep adding paperclips until it floats just right, but be sure the ceiling fan is off. When the balloon doesn't drift up or down and floats, you have achieved 'Equilibrium', just like a fish in an aquarium. They can swim up and not slow down and swim down without speeding up. That's why Buddy couldn't keep up with Dove when she flew down to the waves. (Re: Pg 14)

Made in the USA
Lexington, KY
15 November 2018